Eating by myself...

Making music.

... is fun.

All gone!

My first birthday.

First U.S. edition

LOC NO. 88-80342

10 9 8 7 6 5 4 3 2 1

Joy Street Books are published by
Little, Brown and Company (Inc.)

Printed in Hong Kong

WHEN I WAS A
BABY

Catherine Anholt

Joy Street Books

LITTLE, BROWN AND COMPANY

BOSTON · TORONTO

"What's that, Mom?"
"It's a baby shirt."
"Was it *mine?*
  Was I really that small?"
"Even smaller!"

"When we brought you back
from the hospital, you were
no bigger than a doll."

"What did I eat when I was a baby?"
"For a long time you only drank milk."
"Didn't I even eat cookies?"
"You couldn't — you didn't have any teeth!"

"Is that me, sleeping in that little basket?"
"Yes, and look at all your toys!
  All our friends and relatives came
  to see you, and they brought you
  lots of presents."

"When you were a baby,
   Daddy used to give you a bath
   in that red plastic tub."
"Did I ever splash him?"
"All the time! Poor Daddy was wet
   from head to toe!"

"When I was a baby I wore diapers, didn't I?"
"Yes. And when they were wet you used to
 cry until we changed them —
 even in the middle of the night!"

"When I was a baby,
   did you ever take me for walks?"
"You loved to ride in your carriage.
   Daddy and I took you everywhere."

"When you were big enough, you had
   your own chair, so that you could sit
   at the table with us."
"Did I ever make a mess when I ate my
   dinner?"
"Of course you did. All babies do!"

"Was I a noisy baby?"
"You certainly were!
   As soon as you could sit up,
   your favorite game was banging
   on a saucepan with a wooden spoon."

"I remember one day
  you got lost in the garden.
  You'd crawled right off the blanket.
  You cried and cried."
"What happened then?"
"I came and found you!"

"Did I ever have a party when I was a baby?"
"You did when you turned one.
   All your friends came over
   and I made you a special birthday cake."

"I'm not one now!"
"No. Now you're three."
"I'm not a baby anymore.
   Now I'm three, I'm big!"

My first day home.

Learning to crawl.

At the Beach.

Walking!